The Tiara Club

at Diamond Turrets

For Princess Kasia of Poland,
kochająca, Vivian xxx
VF
With very special thanks to JD

www.tiaraclub.co.uk

ORCHARD BOOKS
338 Euston Road, London NW1 3BH
Orchard Books Australia
Level 17/207 Kent St, Sydney, NSW 2000

A Paperback Original
First published in Great Britain in 2009
Text © Vivian French 2009
Cover illustration © Sarah Gibb 2009
Inside illustrations © Orchard Books 2009

A CIP catalogue record for this book is available
from the British Library.

ISBN 978 1 84616 879 6

1 3 5 7 9 10 8 6 4 2

Printed in Great Britain

The paper and board used in this paperback are natural recyclable products
made from wood grown in sustainable forests. The manufacturing processes
conform to the environmental regulations of the country of origin.

Orchard Books is a division of Hachette Children's Books,
an Hachette UK company

www.hachette.co.uk

The Tiara Club

at Diamond Turrets

Princess Abigail

and the Baby Panda

By Vivian French

ORCHARD BOOKS

The Royal Palace Academy
for the Preparation of Perfect Princesses

(Known to our students as "*The Princess Academy*")

OUR SCHOOL MOTTO:
*A Perfect Princess always thinks of others
before herself, and is kind, caring and truthful.*

Diamond Turrets offers a complete education for
Tiara Club princesses, focusing on caring for animals
and the environment. The curriculum includes:

A visit to the Royal County Show	*Visits to the Country Park and Bamboo Grove*
Work experience on our very own farm	*Elephant rides in our Safari Park (students will be closely supervised)*

Our headteacher, King Percy, is present at all times, and
students are well looked after by Fairy G, the school
Fairy Godmother.

Our resident staff and visiting experts include:

*LADY WHITSTABLE KENT
(IN CHARGE OF THE FARM,
COUNTRY PARK AND SAFARI PARK)*

*QUEEN MOTHER MATILDA
(ETIQUETTE, POSTURE AND
APPEARANCE)*

*FAIRY ANGORA
(ASSISTANT FAIRY GODMOTHER)*

*FARMER KATE
(DOMESTIC ANIMALS)*

*LADY MAY (SUPERVISOR OF THE
HOLIDAY HOME FOR PETS)*

We award tiara points to encourage our Tiara Club princesses towards the next level. All princesses who win enough points at Diamond Turrets will be presented with their Diamond Sashes and attend a celebration ball.

Diamond Sash Tiara Club princesses are invited to return to Golden Gates, our magnificent mansion residence for Perfect Princesses, where they may continue their education at a higher level.

PLEASE NOTE:
Princesses are expected to arrive at the Academy with a *minimum* of:

TWENTY BALLGOWNS
(with all necessary hoops, petticoats, etc)

TWELVE DAY DRESSES

SEVEN GOWNS suitable for garden parties and other special day occasions

TWELVE TIARAS

DANCING SHOES five pairs

VELVET SLIPPERS three pairs

RIDING BOOTS two pairs

Wellington boots, waterproof cloaks and other essential protective clothing as required

Hello! My name's Abigail - what's yours?
And isn't it fun being
here at Diamond Turrets?
I absolutely LOVE it, even though the
twins can be really horrible sometimes.
I don't mind, though. I've got lovely Mia,
Bethany, Caitlin, Lindsey and Rebecca
to keep me company - and you're
here too, which is wonderful!

Chapter One

Do you have morning assemblies at your school? We have them three times a week at Diamond Turrets, and they're really exciting. Sometimes our headteacher, King Percy, tells us how all the different animals are getting on, and sometimes Lady Whitstable-Kent has a new project for us. Lady

Whit's in charge of the country park, the farm and the animals, and she can be just a little bit terrifying. Lindsey says she's very nice and kind when you get to know her, but I'm not sure I really want to try.

Anyway, it was Lady Whit's turn to take assembly, and she came to the front of the platform with a HUGE smile on her face.

"Dear princesses," she began, "I have some wonderful news for you. King Percy and I have been keeping a very special secret for three whole months, but now at last we can tell you. Some of you will have noticed the beautiful bamboo groves at the far end of our country park, and you may even have wondered what we keep there." Lady Whit stopped, and looked at us. "Does anyone here know which animal likes to eat bamboo shoots?"

At once Lindsey's hand shot up. "Please, Lady Whit – pandas!"

Lady Whit beamed at her. "Well done, Princess Lindsey. And we are lucky enough to have a panda here at Diamond Turrets. Three months ago she had a baby, and I'm delighted to say that both mother and baby are doing extremely well. In fact, they are doing SO well that King Percy and I think we can allow you to see them."

Of course we all started talking at once – we were SO excited! We knew there was a huge bamboo grove at the far end of the country park, but nobody had EVER guessed there was a panda there, let alone a panda with a baby! Diamonde jumped to her feet. "Lady Whit, when can we go? Can we go at once?"

I thought Lady Whit would be cross, but she went on smiling. "Yes, Princess Diamonde. You will indeed be seeing the pandas today. As it happens, I've devised a delightful little project for you. Listen carefully! The pandas are in a special enclosure overlooked by

a hide. You will be able to watch them, but they won't see you." Lady Whit stopped smiling, and looked very stern. "I must impress upon you all the importance of NOT letting the mother panda see you. It could frighten her, and she might decide to reject her baby."

Diamonde jumped up again. "If you please, Lady Whit, the panda wouldn't be frightened of ME. Mummy says Gruella and I are the most sensitive girls in the whole wide world."

Lady Whit didn't look at all impressed. "That may be true, Princess Diamonde," she said, "but if you aren't prepared to obey my rules you will not be allowed anywhere near the enclosure."

Diamonde made an angry snorting noise, but she didn't say anything else. Lady Whit gave her a last chilly stare, and then went on, "You will each be given a map of the bamboo grove. There are several interesting plants to be seen, and many butterflies and birds. If you follow the route I have marked you will have a fascinating time, and will also learn more about the conditions in which pandas live. Once you reach the hide you'll find Fairy G waiting for you. She will check that you have come the correct way, and will show you what to do next."

Our school fairy godmother was sitting at the side of the platform, and she nodded at us cheerfully. "There will be a picnic lunch afterwards, my dears. We'll have such a fun day!"

Chapter Two

We couldn't stop talking as we hurried along to the cloakrooms to get ready.

"I adore pandas," Rebecca said. "They're just so cute!"

Lindsey grinned. "They may look cute," she said, "but they've got ever such strong teeth and jaws." She saw us looking at her in surprise, and she laughed. "I had a toy giant panda when I was little, and my mum used to tell me about the real ones. Did you know they're picky about what sort of bamboo they eat?"

"Are they really?" Caitlin asked. "I thought they ate any old bamboo."

Lindsey shook her head. "That's why they're in such danger. They have favourite types of bamboo shoots...but every so often they change their minds. Sometimes they won't eat even when they're surrounded by bamboo shoots!"

Diamonde and Gruella pushed

past us to get to their shoe lockers, and Diamonde stuck her nose in the air. "I see you're showing off again, Lindsey know-it-all!"

Lindsey pretended she hadn't heard, but I got cross. I do know Perfect Princesses are supposed to be forgiving and gracious, but I'm SO not good at it.

"Don't be so horrid and mean," I snapped. "Lindsey knows FAR more about pandas than you do."

Diamonde made a face. "Who wants to know about silly old bears anyway?" she sneered, and flounced away.

Bethany sighed. "I can't believe we're really and truly going to see a real live panda, let alone a baby."

"Come on," Mia said, "or we'll be the last out of school..." And the six of us hurried out of the cloakroom.

We talked about pandas all the way across the country park, and Lindsey told us everything she knew about them. I was SO surprised to hear the babies are born without any fur.

Lindsey giggled. "Mum says they look all pink and wriggly, and they're really, really teeny."

"Do the mothers ever sit on them by mistake?" Bethany asked anxiously, but Lindsey said she didn't think they did.

"Anyway, our baby panda's three months old," she reminded us. "It'll be much bigger, and it'll be just as furry as its mother."

Rebecca sighed happily and said, "I absolutely can't wait to see it."

"Let's run!" Mia suggested, and we tore along the path in the most unprincessy way you can imagine. Of course Lindsey was soon way ahead of us – she can go super- fast in her wheelchair – but she stopped to wait for us

at the gate to the bamboo grove.
Fairy Angora, our assistant fairy
godmother, was standing just
the other side, and she shook her
head at us.

"Don't ever let Lady Whit see you running like that," she told us. "Remember – 'Perfect Princesses are always graceful in every way!' And you need to be quiet from now on."

"Oh, we will be," we promised, and Fairy Angora looked pleased.

"Excellent. Now, here are your maps. You'll see there are six checkpoints along the route; you'll find information cards there for you to to read, and you need to sign your names at each point. Is that quite clear?"

We nodded as we took our maps.

"Good. Now have a lovely time,

and I'll see you later." Fairy Angora fluttered her wings. "Fairy G's picnic is going to be MAGNIFICENT!"

And she waved us on our way.

Mia gave a little skip as we walked along the path that twisted in and out of the towering bamboo. "Isn't she wonderful?"

"Lady Whit would have given us loads of minus tiara points if she

had seen us running," Caitlin agreed. "What do we have to find first on our maps?"

We studied them carefully, and found we had to follow the path until we reached a small pond, where the path divided in two.

It didn't take us long to get there, and we saw a post with an information card on the top. The twins were standing reading it, but when they saw us coming they quickly scribbled their names.

"We don't want to be with THEM," Diamonde said in a very loud voice as they hurried away. "Abigail thinks we're MEAN!"

Chapter Three

As the twins turned a corner and vanished, Rebecca pointed at the map. "Ooops! Aren't they going the wrong way?"

"Diamonde!" I called. "Gruella!" I ran to the corner, but there was no sign of them.

"I can't see them," I reported as I came back to my friends. "Do you think they'll be OK?"

Bethany patted my arm. "Don't worry. They'll soon see they've made a mistake, and find their way to the proper path. Come and sign the check sheet."

I did as she suggested and, after we'd read about the twenty-seven different types of bamboo in the grove, we went on walking. We found the other checkpoints easily, but we didn't see any sign of the twins. The information cards made us feel really pleased with ourselves; they told us lots about pandas, but Lindsey had already shared so much with us there weren't any facts we didn't know.

"Maybe there'll be a test?" Caitlin said hopefully. "We'd be certain to come top, and think how many tiara points we'd win!"

Mia laughed. "I've never heard you actually WANT to do a test before, Caitlin."

"It would probably be about bamboo," Lindsey told them, "and then we'd come bottom."

"Look!" Mia pointed to a weird-looking hut built on a platform high above our heads. "That must be the hide!"

Bethany nodded. "And Fairy G's waiting for us – I can see her boots! Oooooh!" She made an enthusiastic squeaking noise. "We're actually here at last!"

Lindsey looked worried. "I'll never be able to get up there," she said anxiously, but as she spoke Fairy G leant over the balustrade above us. She waved her wand;

a shower of sparkling stars drifted down – and a tall man dressed in a black coat stepped out from the shade.

"Princess Lindsey?" he asked, and when Lindsey nodded he swept her a low bow...and lifted her out of her wheelchair as if she weighed nothing at all.

He actually ran up the steps with her, while we puffed behind – they were VERY steep. There was a fold-up wheelchair waiting for her on the platform, and the man grinned as he settled her into it.

"I'll be back to carry you safely down, Your Highness," he said. Lindsey thanked him, and Fairy G beamed her huge cheerful smile at us.

"Well done, Tulip Room! Now, if you don't mind waiting here for a moment, I'll just make sure

the princesses inside have seen enough. There's only room for six of you at a time, and Rose and Daffodil Room were in front of you." She waved a hand, and we saw all our friends from Rose Room making their way to the other end of the platform.

"That's clever," Mia said. "Look! One set of stairs to come up, and another set to go down."

I didn't answer. I was staring over the edge of the balustrade, hardly daring to breathe. The pillars supporting the platform were at the edge of a small clearing which was surrounded by a glass wall; beyond the wall the bamboo grew tall and thick. From where I was standing the hide blocked most of my view, but I could just see a corner of the clearing...and a large furry black-and-white back. It was the mother panda!

I was about to tell Caitlin, who was standing next to me, when I noticed the bamboo beyond the glass wall was swaying to and fro and – for just a second – I saw Gruella. It was such a tiny glimpse I almost thought I'd imagined it, but at that moment the mother panda made a strange snorting noise and lumbered to her feet.

Chapter Four

I couldn't believe it. The twins must have gone on along the wrong path, and now they were about to appear right in front of the mother panda. What if they scared her away from her baby? She was already peering from side to side as if she sensed someone was near. I absolutely HAD to do something.

I didn't stop to tell anyone what I'd seen. I hurled myself back down the steps, and began pushing my way through the bamboo as quietly as I could. The leaves were horribly sharp, and every step was really hard work – but I forced myself to keep going. I just had to find

the twins, but I didn't want to call out in case that made things worse.

Lindsey had told us that pandas don't see very well, but they have fantastic hearing. On and on I went, until I pushed my way past a particularly thick clump – and I thought I could hear whispering.

I stopped to listen, and then –
WHOOOOOOOMPH!!!

A wind was whistling in my ears, and I was spinning round and round and round. It felt as if I was in the middle of a wild tornado...and then it all went deathly quiet.

I opened my eyes, and I was on the platform in front of the hide. Fairy G was in front of me, and she was ENORMOUS.

"Abigail!" she said, and even though her voice wasn't much louder than a whisper, she sounded so angry my legs turned to jelly. "WHATEVER did you think you were doing? Another few steps and you'd have been

RIGHT in front of the glass wall!"

"I'm...I'm so very, very sorry..."
I stuttered, and as I apologised
I suddenly realised what I'd done.

I'd broken all the rules, but I couldn't tell Fairy G it was because I was trying to warn Diamonde and Gruella. That would have been telling tales, and a Perfect Princess NEVER tells tales.

"If I hadn't brought you back here by magic who KNOWS what would have happened!" Fairy G's face was turning purple, and I took a nervous step backwards as she went on. "I was inside the hide when I saw the mother panda stand up...and two minutes later I saw you fighting your way through the bamboo! I've sent

ALL of the other princesses STRAIGHT back to Diamond Turrets, including your friends from Tulip Room. They were extremely disappointed, as you can imagine. I do hope you realise what a VERY terrible thing you have done!"

What could I say? I hung my head, and stared at the floor.

I was completely miserable. I didn't even look up when I heard feet coming up the steps behind me, and Diamonde's tinkling laugh.

"Goodness me! Could Princess Abigail be in trouble? Fancy that, Gruella! Do you think she's been MEAN to someone?"

Gruella sniggered, but Fairy G cut her short. "Diamonde and Gruella? Why are you here?"

"Oh dear! Are we a little bit late?" Diamonde sounded SO pleased with herself. "I'm sorry, Fairy G. We've been studying the information at the checkpoints VERY carefully."

"Really, Diamonde?" There was a change in Fairy G's voice that made me look up. She was still huge, but now she was staring at the twins in the scariest way. "Is that so? Please tell me – did you

meet any princesses making their way back to Diamond Turrets?"

Diamonde gave another tinkling laugh. "Oh no," she said. "We haven't seen anyone at all, have we, Gruella?"

Gruella shook her head. "Nobody at all."

"I see." Fairy G sounded so grim my knees immediately went back to feeling like jelly. "So you didn't meet anyone – even though every single princess is, at this precise moment, walking back to school along the path you should have been on!"

Chapter Five

There was a very long silence.

Fairy G folded her enormous arms, and glared at the twins. "If you weren't on the path, where EXACTLY were you?"

Diamonde looked Gruella, and Gruella looked at Diamonde, but neither of them said anything. There was another silence, until

Fairy G turned to me. "Can YOU tell me where the twins were, Abigail?"

I could feel myself blushing, and I didn't know what to do. I couldn't tell a fib, but on the other hand I couldn't tell tales.

Fairy G sighed heavily, and waved her wand. At once there was a shower of tiny silver stars, and Fairy Angora was standing on the platform looking extremely surprised.

"You called me?" she asked.

Fairy G nodded. "Could you please tell me if the twins have signed their names on every check sheet?"

Fairy Angora shuffled the papers she was carrying, then looked at them again more closely.

"They've signed the first one," she said, "but none of the others."

"And Abigail?" Fairy G's eyes were glinting.

"She's signed every one," Fairy Angora reported.

Fairy G swung round. "I think I'm beginning to understand. Abigail! Am I right in thinking you saw the twins from up here and then – rather foolishly, but with the best of intentions – went to try and stop them from scaring the pandas?"

I stood on one foot, and felt myself blushing even more.

"I'll take that as a yes," Fairy G boomed, and Gruella gave a shriek of protest.

"We weren't going to SCARE the pandas," she said. "Diamonde said they'd LOVE us, because we're special. But then we saw Abigail running down the steps—" Gruella stopped dead as Diamonde trod heavily on her foot. "OUCH! That really HURT, Diamonde!"

Fairy G didn't exactly wave her wand, but she gave it a tiny flick – and although Diamonde opened her mouth, not a single word came out.

"Go on, Gruella," Fairy G said.

Gruella gave a nervous giggle. "We decided to run away from Abigail, but all of a sudden she vanished." Gruella frowned. "It was WEIRD. One minute she was right beside us, and the next minute – *whoosh!* She was gone!"

Fairy G put her hand on my shoulder, and I absolutely knew everything was all right again.

"Abigail, my dear," she said, "I apologise. Run into the hide, and tell me what those pandas are up to. Fairy Angora – would you be kind enough to take the twins back to school? Tell Lady Whitstable-Kent and King Percy everything. Oh, and please send the princesses back to the country park...I can't have my beautiful picnic going to waste!"

As the twins trailed away behind Fairy Angora, I tiptoed into the hide. It was AMAZING! There was a glass floor, and I could see the mother panda snuggling up with her baby, and licking the top of its head. They looked SO happy!

A moment later Fairy G came to find me.

"They look splendid, don't they?" she said.

I nodded. "I do hope they weren't too scared."

Fairy G laughed a huge booming laugh. I jumped, but the pandas took no notice at all. "It's amazing what a little soothing magic can do," she told me, and then she winked. "Quite soon the little one will be crawling about, and they'll need more room. We'll let them out into the bamboo grove, but we'll need a kind and thoughtful princess to help look after them.

Do you think that you might be interested?"

"Oh YES," I breathed. "Yes, PLEASE!" And I had a thought.

"Dear Fairy G – could my friends help as well? PLEASE?"

"Consider it done." Fairy G smiled her amazing smile. "And now, I think it's time for Tulip Room to take their turn watching

the pandas. But don't be too long!
There's a simply wonderful picnic
waiting for you!"

And as Fairy G stomped away,
I saw my friends hurrying in the
other door looking SO excited.

"Abigail!" Mia said, and gave me a huge hug. "We were so worried about you!"

"I'm fine," I said. "Come and see the pandas!" And we stood in a row and gazed and gazed at the mother and baby as they cuddled up together.

Chapter Six

Fairy G's picnic was utterly FANTASTIC. There were so many different kinds of sandwiches we lost count, and the cakes were unbelievably delicious. After we'd eaten we sat down on silvery cushions and soft woollen rugs, and Fairy G told us stories about giant pandas. She waved her wand,

and stars floated up...and then, as they settled, we could actually *see* pictures of pandas swimming in

a lake, playing in the snow, and
even doing somersaults! It was
completely magical.

We were still talking about it as we got ready for bed later that evening, and about how gorgeous the mother and baby were.

"And I've got a very special surprise," I said as we snuggled down. "Fairy G wants us to help look after the baby panda when it's bigger."

All five of my friends sat bolt upright in bed and stared at me, their eyes open wide. "REALLY?" they said. "Are you sure?"

I had to swear on my honour it was true before they'd believe me, and then they gave me such a loud cheer that Fairy G came and opened the door to tell us to be quiet.

"HUSH!" she boomed. "HUSH! Or you won't be looking after that baby panda after all..."

But she winked as she closed the door, so we knew she didn't mean it.

Bethany puffed up her pillow, and smiled at me. "Aren't friends just so wonderful?" she said. "Abigail – you're the best!"

And do you know what? You're the best friend ever as well!